This book belongs to:

. . . .

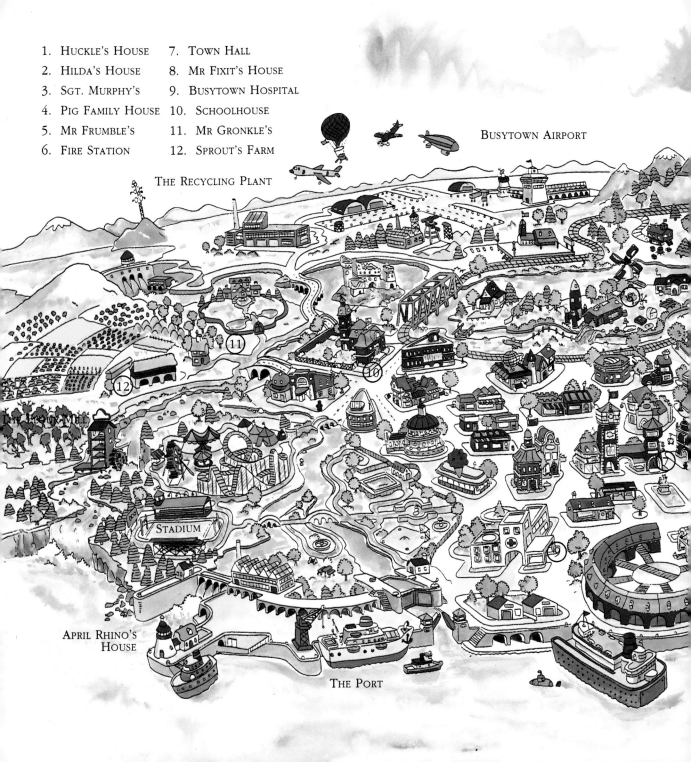

1. HUCKLE'S HOUSE
2. HILDA'S HOUSE
3. SGT. MURPHY'S
4. PIG FAMILY HOUSE
5. MR FRUMBLE'S
6. FIRE STATION
7. TOWN HALL
8. MR FIXIT'S HOUSE
9. BUSYTOWN HOSPITAL
10. SCHOOLHOUSE
11. MR GRONKLE'S
12. SPROUT'S FARM

BUSYTOWN AIRPORT

THE RECYCLING PLANT

STADIUM

APRIL RHINO'S
HOUSE

THE PORT

MOUNT BUSY
OBSERVATORY

SKI CHALET

Welcome to
Busytown!

CAMPING GROUNDS

BUSY BAY
POINT

BRUNO'S
SNACK
STAND

① ④ ②

⑥ ③

THE BEACH

THE
TRAIN
STATION

BUSYTOWN GRAND HOTEL

SEA FORT

First published in Great Britain in 1995
by HarperCollins Publishers Ltd,
77-85 Fulham Palace Road,
Hammersmith, London W6 8JB
1 3 5 7 9 10 8 6 4 2
Copyright © 1995 The Estate of Richard Scarry
Adapted from the animated television series
The Busy World of Richard Scarry ™
produced by Paramount Pictures and Cinar
All rights reserved.
ISBN: 0 00 664569 0
Printed and bound in Italy
Designed and produced by Les Livres du Dragon d'Or

The Busy World of Richard Scarry

Billy Dog's Bad Day

Collins

An Imprint of HarperCollinsPublishers

Lowly Worm, Huckle Cat and Sally Cat are going to school in the school bus.

"Have you heard?" says Lynnie. "There's someone new starting school today. His name is Bully. Bully Dog!"

"With a name like Bully, he can't be very nice," says Huckle.

"Never judge a book by its cover!" remarks Lowly.

"I'm sure his name's not really Bully," says Hilda Hippo. "He's probably a sweet little boy."

"Look, there he is!" she shouts.

The children stare at
their new classmate.
"He really doesn't look
very nice," says Lowly.

The new pupil gets on
the bus and takes a seat
behind Huckle and Lowly.
All the children are silent.
They are afraid of him.

"Maybe he's nice once you
get to know him," Huckle
whispers to Lowly.

"Yes, maybe Huckle. You go and get to know him and I'll just wait here," suggests Lowly.

Huckle walks over to the new boy's seat. "Hi, Bully Dog, I'm..."

Craaash!

Huckle trips over
Bully Dog's school bag.

Snap! go all the pencils.

"Hey!" Bully Dog shouts.
"You've broken my pencils!"

In the classroom Miss Honey introduces the new boy.
"Children, we have a new pupil today. His name is Billy Dog."

"See!" Hilda whispers to Lynnie. "I KNEW his name wasn't Bully."

"Take a seat next to Huckle, please," Miss Honey says to Billy Dog.

"Oh no! What do I do now?" Huckle asks Lowly.
"Finish school! Quickly!" Lowly says.

Huckle trembles with fear as Billy takes his seat.
"Miss Honey says you're going to help me,"
Billy Dog tells Huckle.
"Oh, of course. Anything
you say," Huckle mutters
nervously.

Miss Honey calls Billy
to the blackboard.
"Billy, can you tell me
what the answer is?"
Billy looks
embarrassed. He
doesn't know the
answer.

Lowly leans towards Huckle.
"Maybe this is your chance
to help him out," he suggests.
"What a good idea, Lowly.
Thanks!" says Huckle.
Huckle raises his hand and calls
out, "The answer's nine, Billy!"

"I could have worked that out for myself!" snaps Billy.
"Now boys, why don't you show me how well you can
work together?" says Miss Honey. "Can you fetch the
geography books, please?"

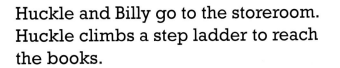

Huckle and Billy go to the storeroom.
Huckle climbs a step ladder to reach
the books.

CRASH! BOOM!

The books fall down on Billy!

The children rush to see what has happened.
"I don't think dumping books on top of Billy is the right way to make friends," Lowly tells Huckle.

Soon it's break time.
Some of the children start a game of football.

Huckle kicks the ball to Lowly

and Lowly kicks it back.

Billy Dog runs over to kick the ball, but he collides with Huckle.

Boom!
Huckle flies through the air...

...and lands in the goal! Billy runs up to Huckle, but Huckle just shouts and runs away!

At lunchtime, Huckle and Lowly go
to the playground to eat their lunch.

Uh oh!
Here comes Billy Dog!
Huckle runs to hide.

Just then, Bananas Gorilla
walks by.

"Come and sit with us, Bananas!" Huckle calls, coming out from behind the bush. "It's your lucky day! Have my banana."

Bananas sits down beside Huckle.

When Billy sees the bench is full, he goes to sit elsewhere.

"You just saved our lives!"
Huckle tells Bananas.

"Oh really? Well, it was a
pleasure," Bananas replies.

Back in the classroom the children are drawing maps of Busytown.

"When you have finished drawing your maps, I'd like you to add your houses," Miss Honey says. But poor Billy can't find his street.
"Huckle, maybe you can help Billy," Miss Honey suggests.

"But Miss Honey," says Huckle, "his name's not Billy... it's BULLY!"

"Why, Huckle! That's a terrible thing to say!" Miss Honey is shocked. "This is Billy's first day in a strange school."

"I'm sorry, Miss Honey," Huckle apologises.

Huckle goes over to Billy. "Bully Dog? I mean Billy... Would you like me to show you where your house goes?"

"Well, it's somewhere on Spring Street."
"Oh! That's right near MY house!" Huckle says, pointing to a spot on the map.

"Really!" says Billy. "Then maybe I could visit you sometime?"

Huckle races back to Lowly. "Now he knows where I LIVE!" he whispers. "Lowly, we will have to move!"

When school is over, the children wait for the school
bus to take them home.

"Hey, Huckle!" Billy calls.
Huckle and Lowly look at Billy nervously.
"Why did you help me in class after you
were so mean to me all day?" Billy Dog asks.
"Me? Mean?" Huckle is amazed.

"Sure! First you broke my pencils. Then you made me feel stupid in class. Then you dropped books on me and made that gorilla scare me. And then when I tried to say sorry on the football pitch, you ran away!"
"I thought it was YOU who was being mean," says Huckle.
"Let's be friends," Lowly says to Billy. "Hi, I'm Lowly Worm."
"And I'm Huckle," says Huckle. "Welcome to Busytown." They all shake hands.

Huckle, Lowly and Billy take the school bus home together.
"Do you want to come to my house to play?" Huckle asks Billy.
"That would be GREAT!" Billy replies.

"I hope you are going to like it here in Busytown," Huckle says to his new friend. "I already do!" Billy laughs.

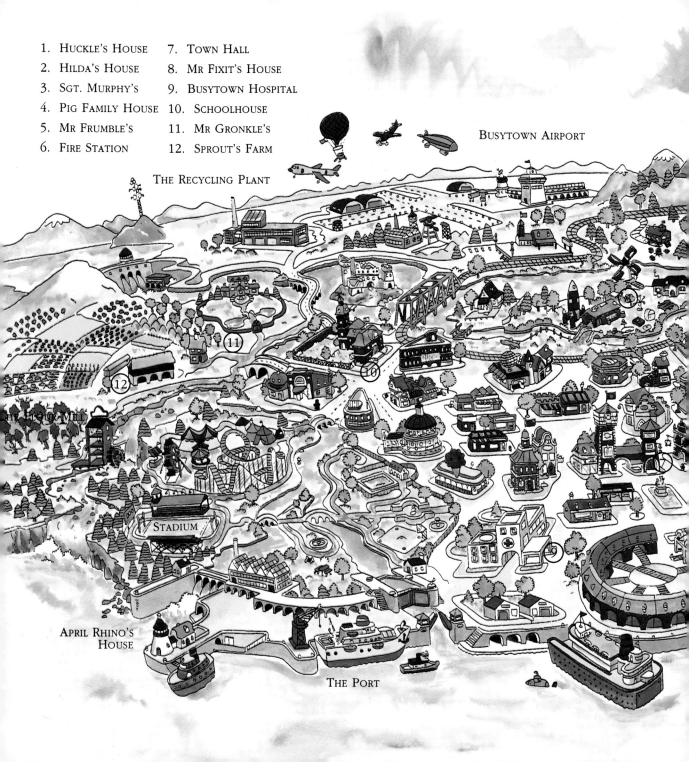

1. HUCKLE'S HOUSE
2. HILDA'S HOUSE
3. SGT. MURPHY'S
4. PIG FAMILY HOUSE
5. MR FRUMBLE'S
6. FIRE STATION
7. TOWN HALL
8. MR FIXIT'S HOUSE
9. BUSYTOWN HOSPITAL
10. SCHOOLHOUSE
11. MR GRONKLE'S
12. SPROUT'S FARM

THE RECYCLING PLANT

BUSYTOWN AIRPORT

STADIUM

APRIL RHINO'S
HOUSE

THE PORT